SERVE TO CHANGE LIVES
In recognition of
Fred Schmechel

Rotary Club of Laramie
2020-2021

WHERE IS BONA BEAR?

MIKE CURATO

GODWINBOOKS

Henry Holt and Company / New York

Tiny was having a big party.
But where was Bina Bear?

Bina?

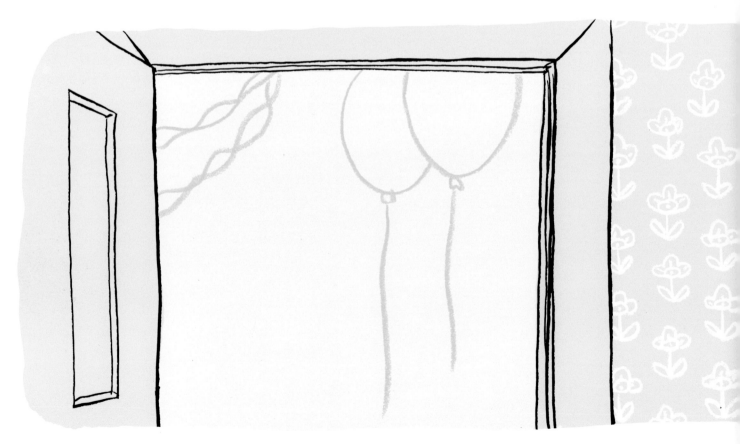

Sigh...

:nom nom nom:

Do you want some banana, tree?

yes.

Bina. What are you doing?

I'm fine.

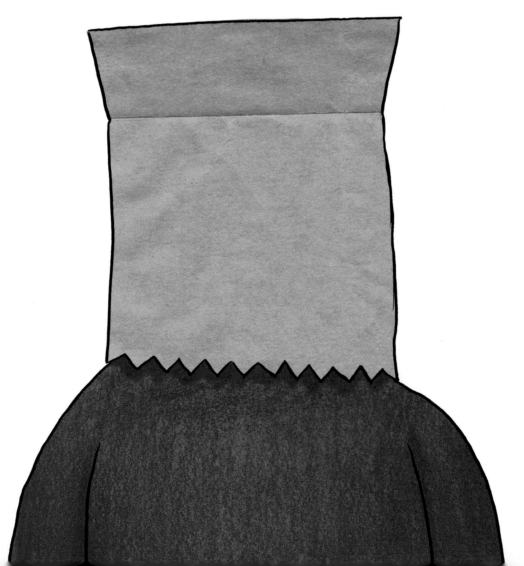

Maybe they're in here!

Where are Tiny and Bina?
I saw them a while ago...

 Hmmm...

'Let's get back to the party.

C'mon,
Spot!

Hmmm...

'Let's get back to the party.

C'mon, Spot!

This book is dedicated to someone who is too shy to name.

Henry Holt and Company, *Publishers since 1866* ❧ Henry Holt® is a registered trademark of Macmillan Publishing Group, LLC. 120 Broadway, New York, NY 10271 ❧ mackids.com ❧ Copyright © 2022 by Mike Curato ❧ All rights reserved ❧ Library of Congress Cataloging-in-Publication Data is available. ❧ ISBN 978-1-250-76220-7 ❧ Our books may be purchased in bulk for promotional, educational, or business use. Please contact your local bookseller or the Macmillan Corporate and Premium Sales Department at (800) 221-7945 ext. 5442 or by email at MacmillanSpecialMarkets@macmillan.com. ❧ First edition, 2022 Book design by Sharismar Rodriguez ❧ Printed in China by RR Donnelley Asia Printing Solutions Ltd., Dongguan City, Guangdong Province ❧ Art is ink, colored pencil, watercolor, and digital.

1 3 5 7 9 10 8 6 4 2